Peter Pan

J.M. Barrie

Level 3

Retold by Marie Crook

Series Editor: Melanie Williams

Once upon a time, in London, there was a little girl, Wendy. She loved reading stories to her brothers, John and Michael. Their favourite stories were about Peter Pan.

1

Peter Pan lived in Neverland with his friends Tinkerbell and the Lost Boys.

'Let's go to Neverland!' said John.
'We can't go to Neverland,' explained Wendy, 'because we can't fly.'

But Peter Pan could fly.
One night he flew to London
with his friend Tinkerbell.
When they flew past an open
window, they heard Wendy
telling the story
about Neverland.

They flew inside. 'Do you want to come to Neverland?' asked Peter Pan.

'Yes!' Wendy cried, 'but we can't fly.' 'It's easy!' said Peter Pan. 'Just think about lovely things!'

4

Michael thought about chocolate,
John thought about holidays and
Wendy thought about her mother.
It was easy!
They began to fly.

'Whee!' they all shouted.
'Let's go!' said Peter Pan.

Soon they were flying over Neverland. It was beautiful. 'We are going to have a brilliant time!' said Peter Pan.

But as soon as he spoke, Wendy began to fall.

The Lost Boys were throwing stones at her. 'Be careful. Peter Pan!' they cried, 'It's a dangerous bird!'

Peter Pan laughed at them and then caught Wendy in his arms.

'You are silly!' he smiled, 'these are our
new friends, Wendy, John and Michael.'
The Lost Boys were silly, but very friendly.
'Let's take them home!' they cried.

The Lost Boys' home was under a tree.
There, Peter described his fights with Hook.
'Hook is a mean pirate,' he said.
'And he hates Peter Pan!'
cried the Lost Boys.

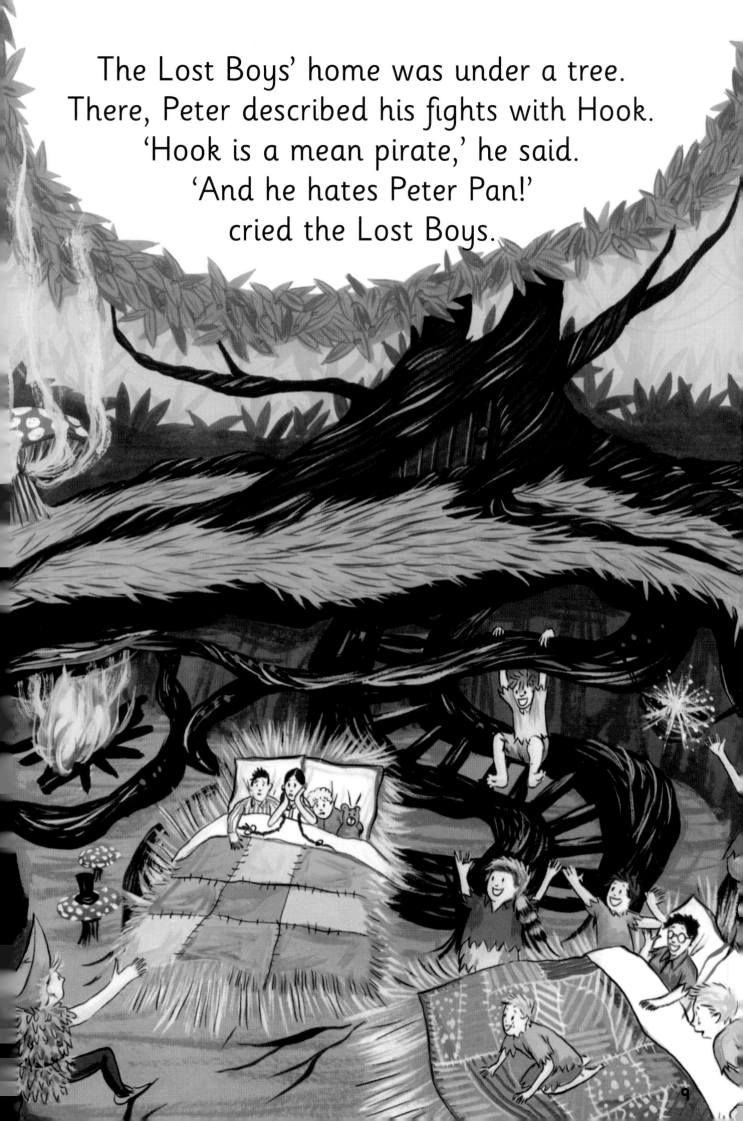

'Years ago,' Peter explained, 'I cut off Hook's hand when we were fighting.'

'Yes,' said the Lost Boys, 'and now Hook has one hand and a hook!'

'I threw the hand to a hungry crocodile!' Peter said, 'and it liked the taste. Now it follows Hook everywhere, because it is hoping to eat more of him!'

When Wendy went to sleep that night she was afraid. But the next day, there were rainbows in the sky.

'Let's go and play with the mermaids today!' said Peter.

When they were playing with the mermaids, they suddenly saw a ship.

They stopped their picnic and looked. 'Hook's here' cried Peter, 'and who has he got?

13

'Ahoy, Peter Pan!'
said Hook, 'I've
got your friend!'
Peter saw that
it was his friend
Tiger Lily.
'Help me Peter!'
Peter flew quickly
to the ship
to help her.

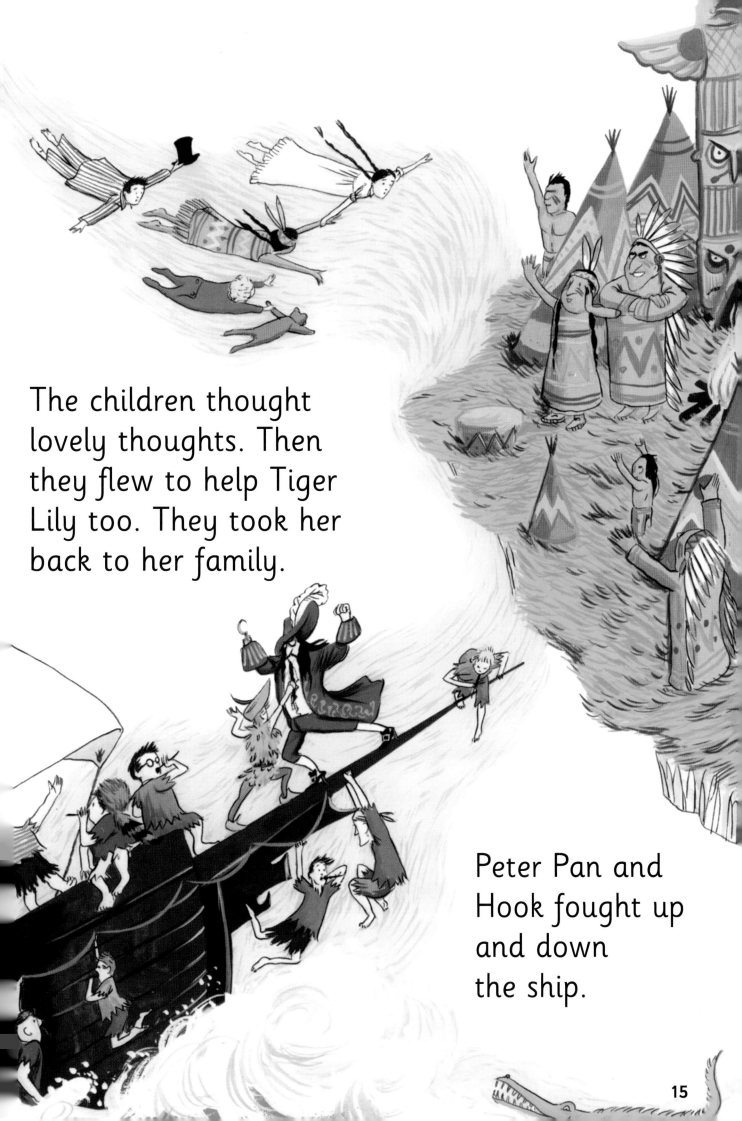

The children thought lovely thoughts. Then they flew to help Tiger Lily too. They took her back to her family.

Peter Pan and Hook fought up and down the ship.

'You will never catch me!' cried Peter. He pushed Hook and then flew away. The crocodile was waiting to catch Hook. 'Aaagh!' cried Hook and he nearly fell into the water.

Hook said to the pirates,
'We must find Peter Pan!'
They walked and walked until
they found the house under the tree.
Peter Pan and the others were there.

The pirates
listened.

'Neverland is too dangerous,' said Wendy,
'let's all go home. I want to see my mother.'
'We have never seen a mother before,' said the
Lost Boys.

They decided to go to Wendy's home. Peter said, 'I'm not coming. I don't want to grow up. If I stay in Neverland, I will always be a little boy!'

The children said goodbye to Peter Pan and started to walk home. But the pirates caught them.

When they all shouted 'Help!' Peter Pan could not hear them.

Hook took the children to his ship. He gave them pirate clothes.

'Now you're my pirates!' he said, 'When Peter Pan comes, we'll fight him together!'

'Never!' they all cried.

Tinkerbell was with the mermaids when she saw the children with Hook.
'Hook's got the children!' she cried, 'I must tell Peter Pan.'

She flew as fast as she could.

Peter Pan went quickly to help the children. 'Hook!' he cried, 'Let's fight!' He climbed the ship's mast.

Hook followed him, higher and higher.

'To catch me' said Peter Pan . . .

. . . You've got to fly!'

But Hook could not fly because he did not have any lovely thoughts.
When Peter flew, Hook fell into the water where the crocodile was waiting.

'We must go home now, Peter,'
said Wendy sadly. 'Remember me.'
'I'll never forget you!' said Peter.

This time, when they wanted
to fly, the children thought
about Peter Pan.

'Goodbye!' they cried
as they flew away.

Wendy's mother was very
happy when she saw them.
She agreed that the Lost
Boys could stay. They stayed
for many, many years.

The boys grew up and they forgot Peter Pan.

But Wendy remembered him.

When she had a daughter, Jane, she described Peter Pan to her.

Peter Pan never forgot Wendy.

Many years later, Peter Pan came to London again.

He was still a little boy! When Jane saw him, she smiled.

Then she thought about her mother, and flew . . .

Before You Read

1. Look at the pictures in Peter Pan. Put a ✓ next to the things you can find in the book.

some mermaids	a castle	a book
a crocodile	a fairy	an ambulance
a forest	a picnic	a ship
some little boys	a pirate	some cats

2. Look at the picture of Neverland. Describe it.

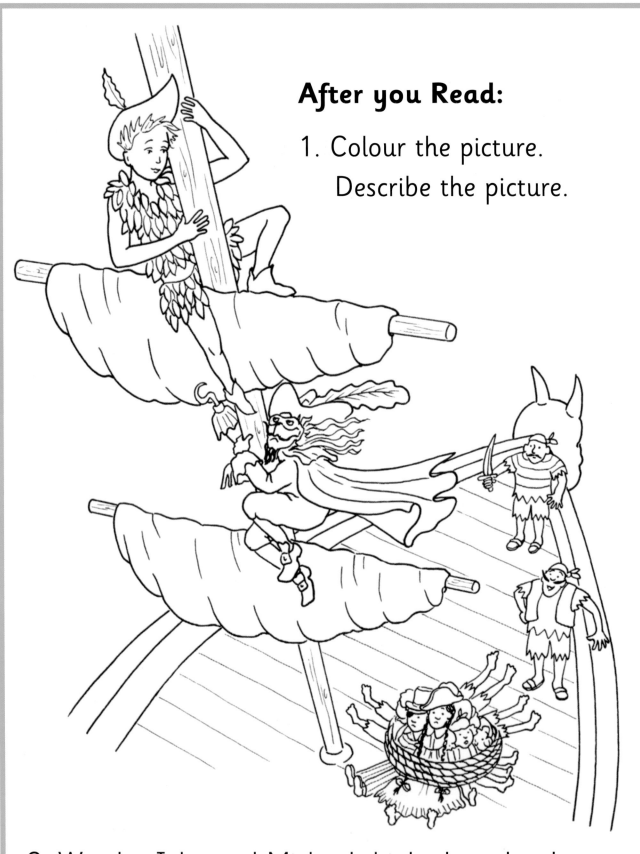

After you Read:

1. Colour the picture.
   Describe the picture.

2. Wendy, John and Michael think about lovely things when they want to fly.
   Think about a lovely thing. Write about it and draw a picture of it.